For E.M. and Y.M. with love

First published in 2005 by Macmillan Children's Books
A division of Macmillan Publishers Limited
20 New Wharf Road, London N1 9RR
Basingstoke and Oxford
Associated companies throughout the world
www.panmacmillan.com

ISBN 1 405 02193 4 (HB)
ISBN 1 405 05153 1 (PB)

Text and illustrations copyright © Rosie Reeve 2005
Moral rights asserted

1 3 5 7 9 8 6 4 2 (HB)
1 3 5 7 9 8 6 4 2 (PB)

A CIP catalogue record for this book
is available from the British Library.

Printed in Belgium by Proost

Rosie Reeve

Cuddle Up Tight!

MACMILLAN CHILDREN'S BOOKS

Every night when I'm ready for bed,
I tuck my teddy up, right here
on my pillow.

Night-night, Teddy.
Cuddle up tight!

But tonight it's stormy outside
and Teddy is scared.

Teddy wants big, brave Spotty Leopard,
because leopards aren't scared of anything.

Night-night, Teddy. Night-night, Spotty Leopard.

Cuddle up tight!

But Spotty Leopard says she can't sleep
without her best friend, Elephant.

Night-night, Teddy. Night-night, Spotty Leopard.
Night-night, Elephant.

Cuddle up tight!

But Elephant says Zebra's not feeling very well.

Open wide, Zebra –
you'll be all better
in the morning!

Night-night, Teddy. Night-night, Spotty Leopard.
Night-night, Elephant. Night-night, Zebra.

Cuddle up tight!

Now everyone wants a bedtime story!

Settle down, please.
It's story time, not
wriggle-about time!

Now it's time to go to sleep.

But Dinosaur's left all on his own.
Don't worry, Dinosaur, we'll fit you in somehow!

There! Now everyone's in:
Teddy, Spotty Leopard, Elephant, Zebra and Dinosaur.

We haven't forgotten
anyone, have we?

Wait!
What about ME?

Everybody out!

Now everyone's cosy again,
so I'll get into bed.

But first I'll just . . .

tuck Teddy up, right here on my pillow,
so I've got someone to cuddle all night!

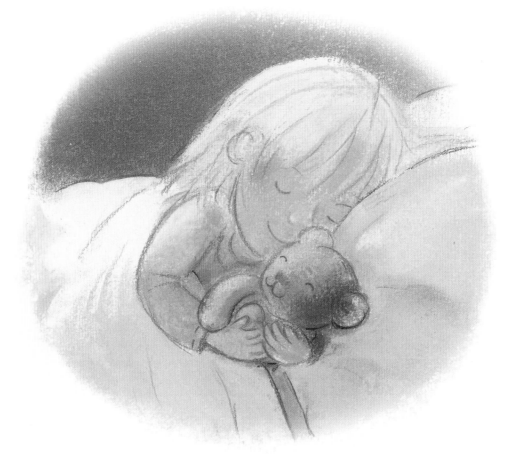

Night-night, Teddy. Night-night, me.
Cuddle up tight!